Owlkids Books Inc.
10 Lower Spadina Avenue, Suite 400, Toronto, Ontario M5V 2Z2
www.owlkids.com

Distributed in Canada by University of Toronto Press
5201 Dufferin Street, Toronto, Ontario M3H 5T8

Distributed in the United States by Publishers Group West
1700 Fourth Street, Berkeley, California 94710

Library and Archives Canada Cataloguing in Publication

Cordier, Séverine
Picture my day / Séverine Cordier and Cynthia Lacroix ; translated by Lesley Zimic.

Translation of: C'est mon imagier.
ISBN 978-1-926973-30-2

1. Vocabulary--Juvenile literature. 2. Word recognition--Juvenile literature.
I. Lacroix, Cynthia II. Zimic, Lesley III. Title.

PE1449.C67 2012 j428.1 C2011-905825-1

Library of Congress Control Number: 2011935959

Canadian Heritage Patrimoine canadien

Canada

Ontario Media Development Corporation
Société de développement de l'industrie des médias de l'Ontario

Canada Council for the Arts Conseil des Arts du Canada

ONTARIO ARTS COUNCIL
CONSEIL DES ARTS DE L'ONTARIO

We acknowledge the financial support of the Canada Council for the Arts, the Government of Canada through the Canada Book Fund, the Ontario Arts Council and the Ontario Media Development Corporation for our publishing activities.

Manufactured by Imago Services (HK) Ltd.
Manufactured in Dongguan City, China, in October 2011
Job # ESF0010A

A B C D E F

Picture my Day

Séverine Cordier • Cynthia Lacroix

It's getting light...

Picture my Day

For Lou-Anne, Max, and Lili-Rose

—Séverine and Cynthia

bed
cot

bunk bed

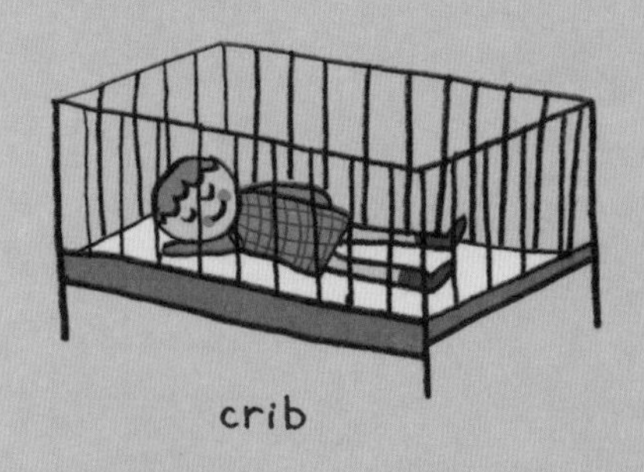
crib

pillows

blanket

sleeper
pajamas

nightgown

Breakfast is served...

teacup

kettle

sippy cups

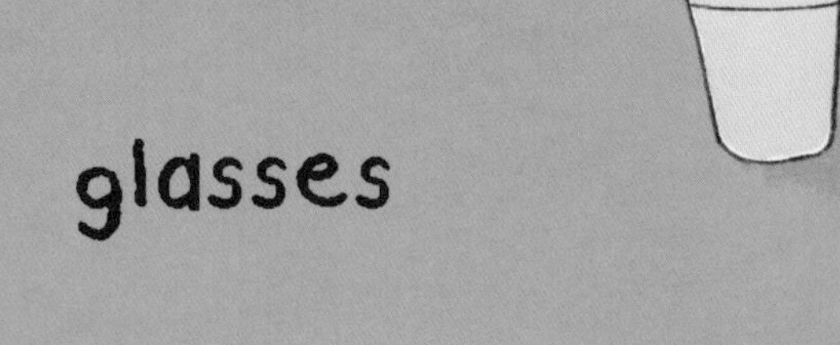

glasses

bowls

cups

milk

plum
cherry
lemon
apple
apricot
blueberry
lime
honey
strawberry
chocolate
marmalade
grape
blackberry
black currant
raspberry
cranberry

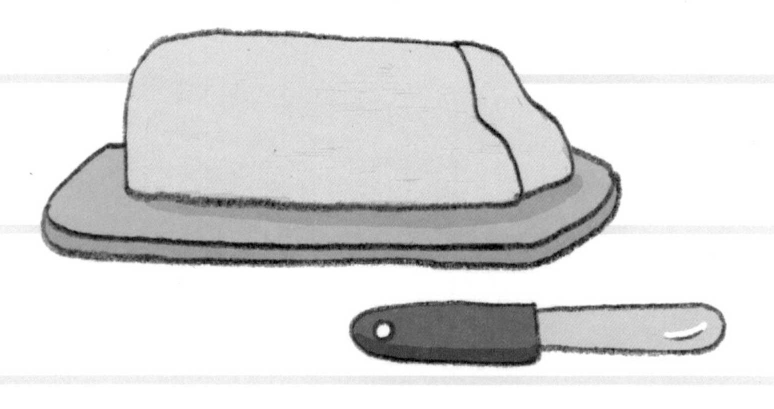

butter

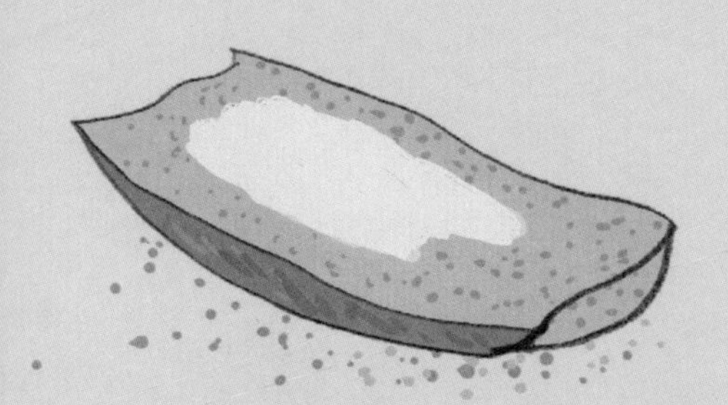

toast

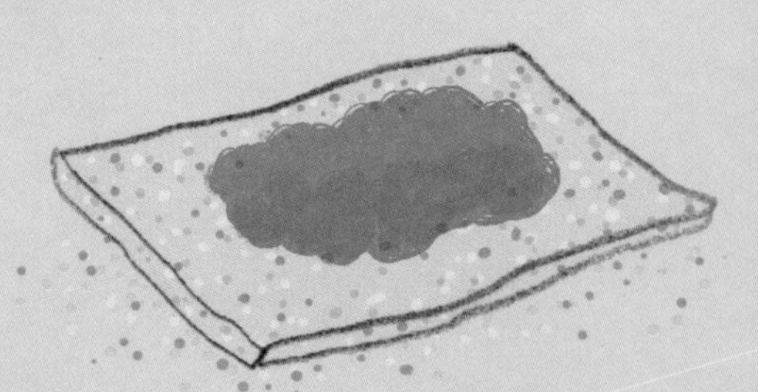

From head to toe...

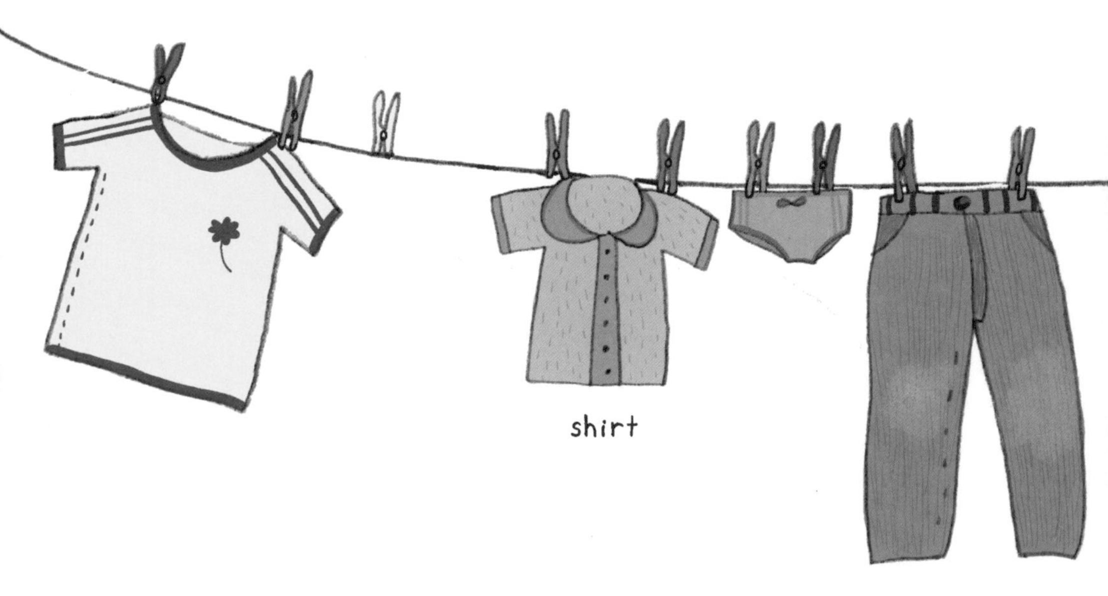
shirt
jeans

sweater
overalls

green sock
red T-shirt

yellow onesie
blue tank top

polka-dot cardigan
checked overalls

striped sweater
flowery jacket

playing dress-up

socks

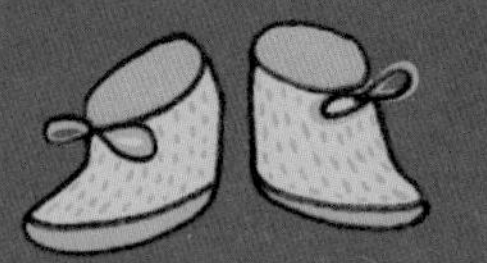

slippers

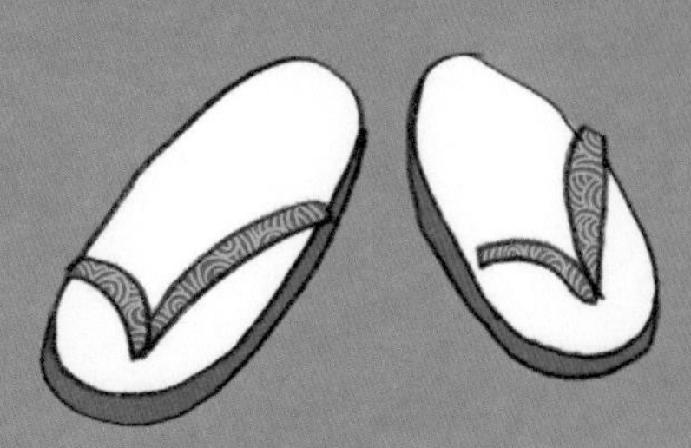

laundry basket

washing machine

toothbrushes

brush
brush

combing

sulking

diaper
potty

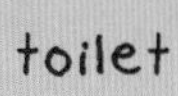

toilet

Time to play...

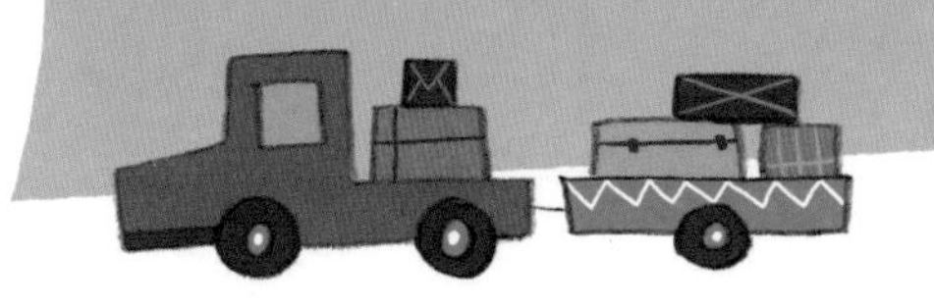

toy cars

teddy bear

stuffies

blocks

bookcase

books

story time

dolls

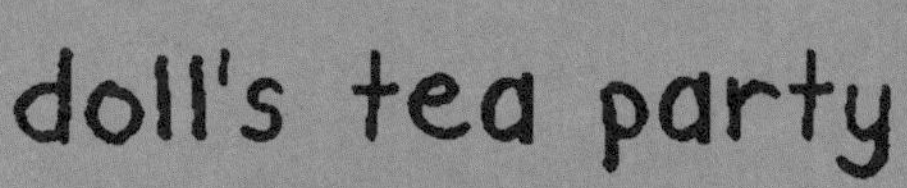
doll's tea party

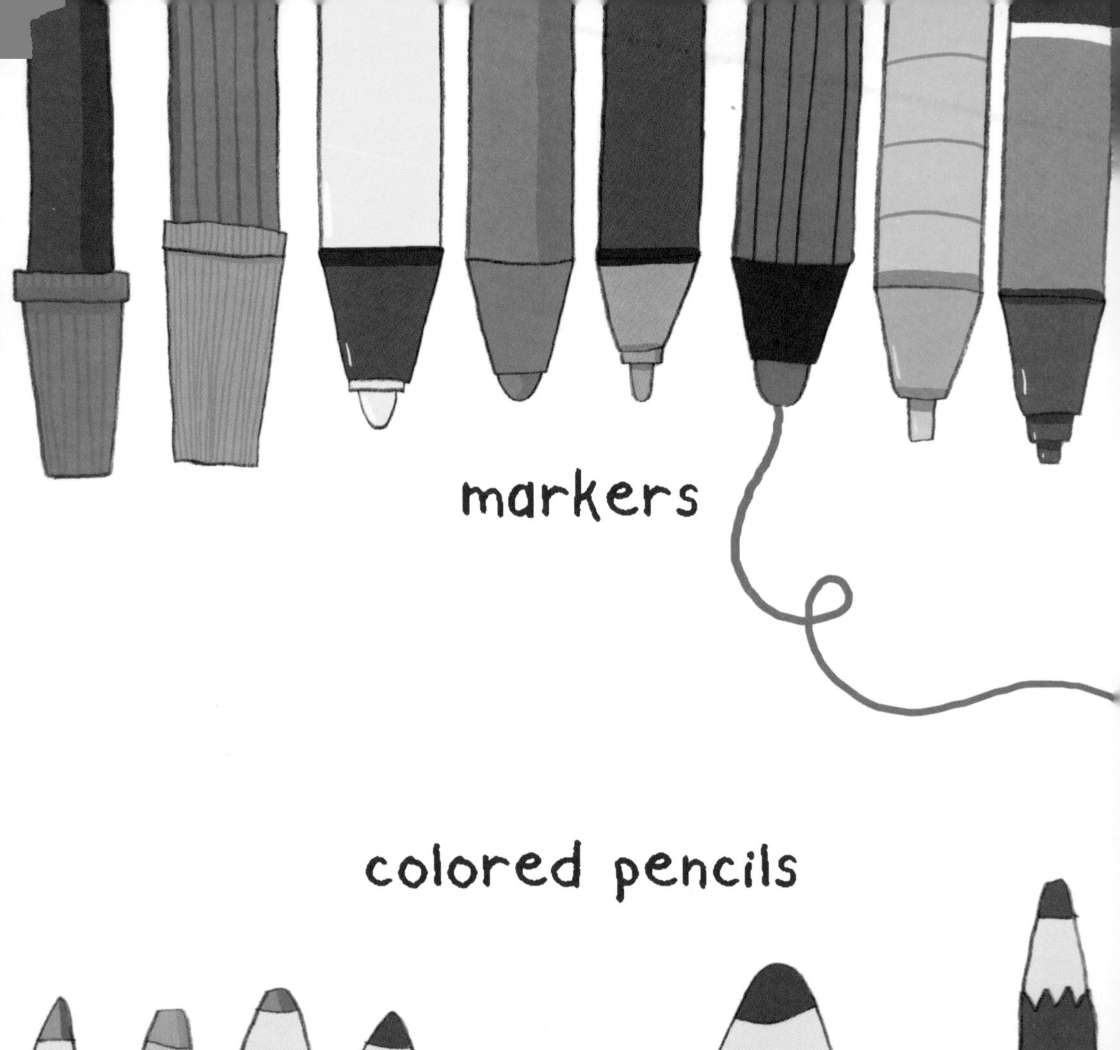
markers
colored pencils

being naughty

tom-toms
keyboard
maracas
recorder
tambourine

drum
xylophone

modeling clay

jigsaw puzzle

Let's take a walk...

in the hall

Mommy's purse

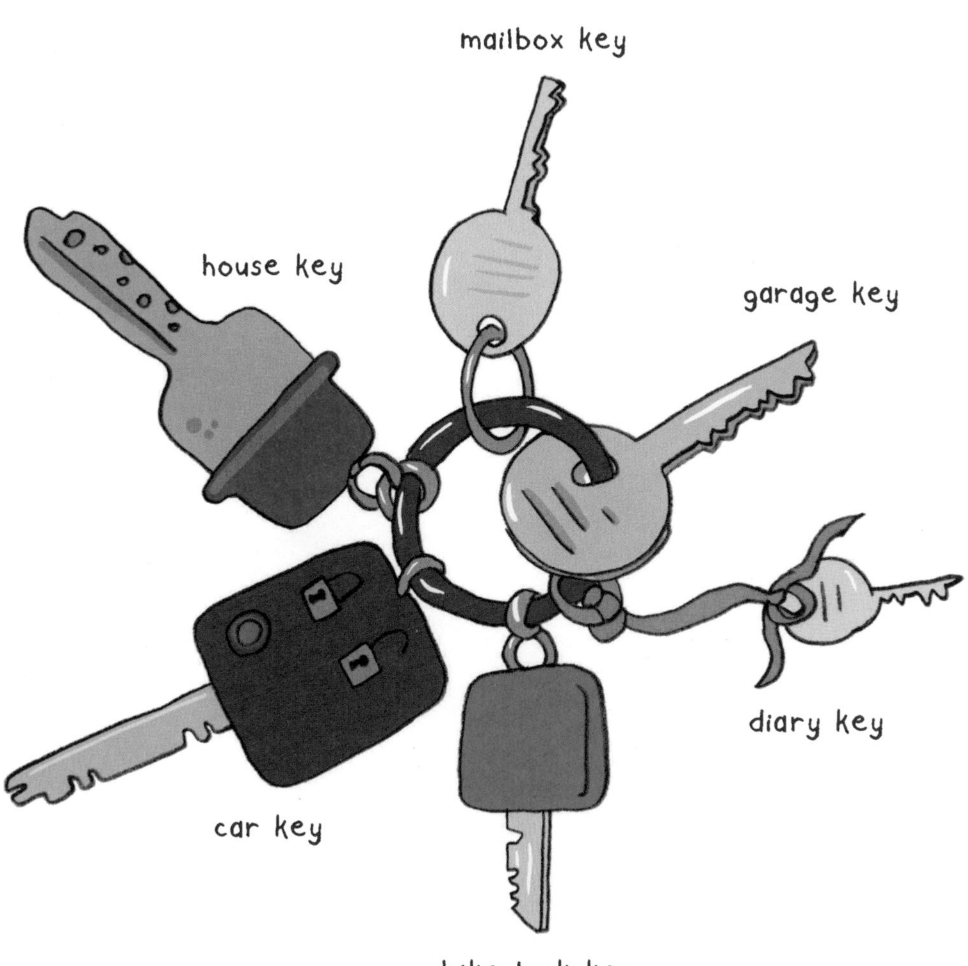
mailbox key
house key
garage key
diary key
car key
bike lock key

key chain

on the street

garbage truck

fire truck

scooter

motorcycle

looking for adventure

stroller

scooter

park

playground

sandbox

pebbles and stones

hopscotch

market

checkout

visiting neighbors

Time to eat...

cupboard

pasta
rice
lentils
sardines
CHOCOLAT
sugar
honey

strainer
bread knife
pie server
cheese grater
ladle

parents' cutlery

children's cutlery

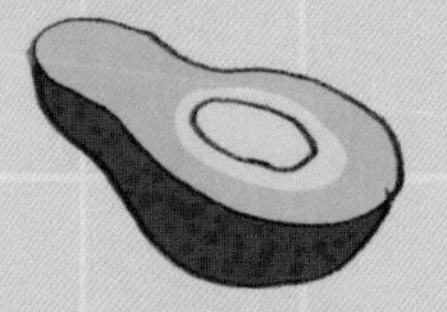

avocado

green beans

tomato

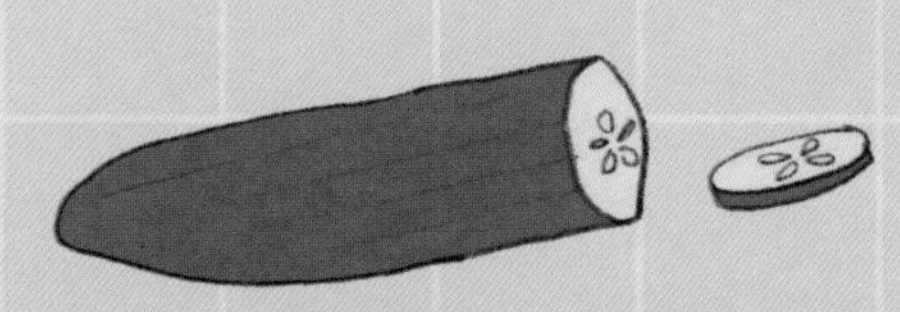

cucumber

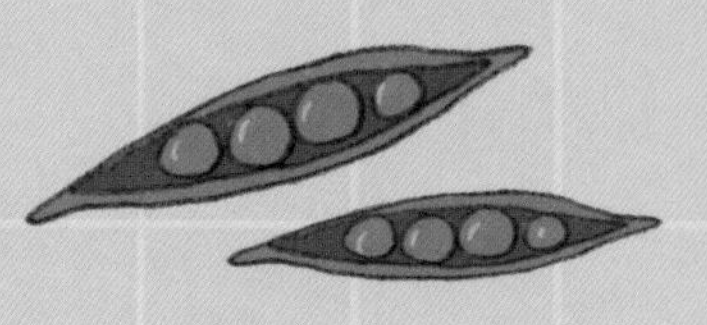

peas

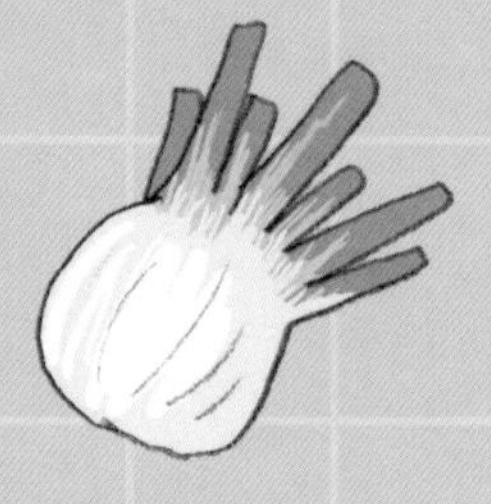

fennel

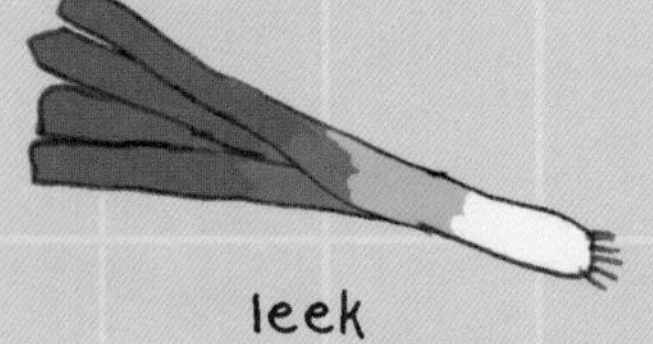

leek

broccoli

radishes

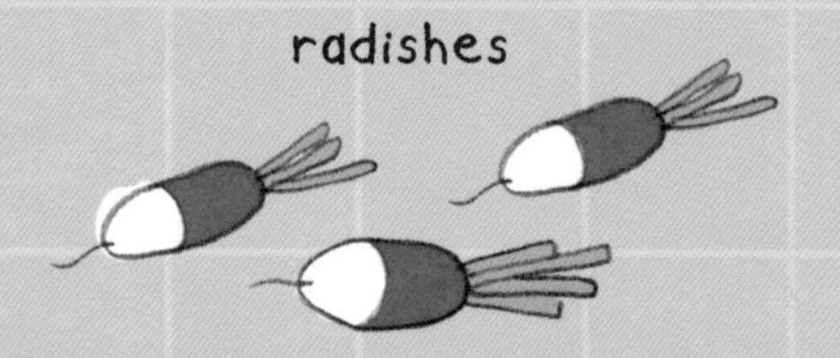

beet

basil

corn

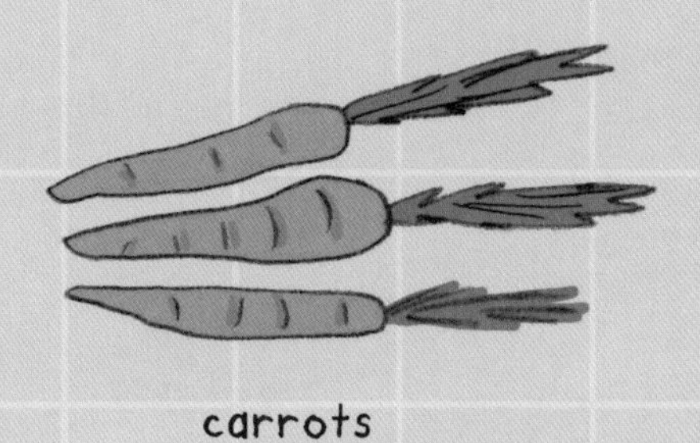

carrots

sweet pepper

cherry tomatoes

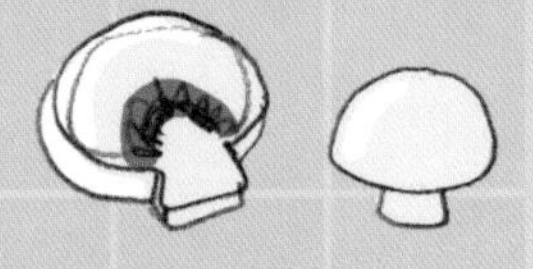

mushrooms

artichoke

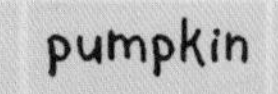

pumpkin

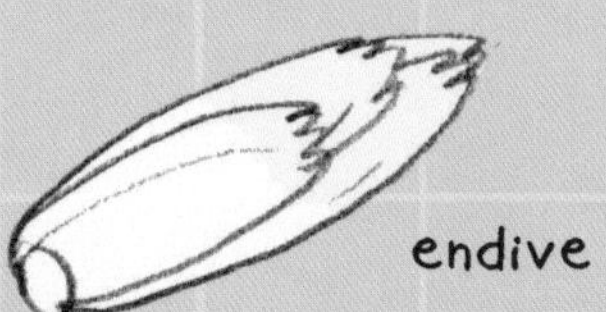

endive

ham
fried egg
breaded fish
hamburger

stew

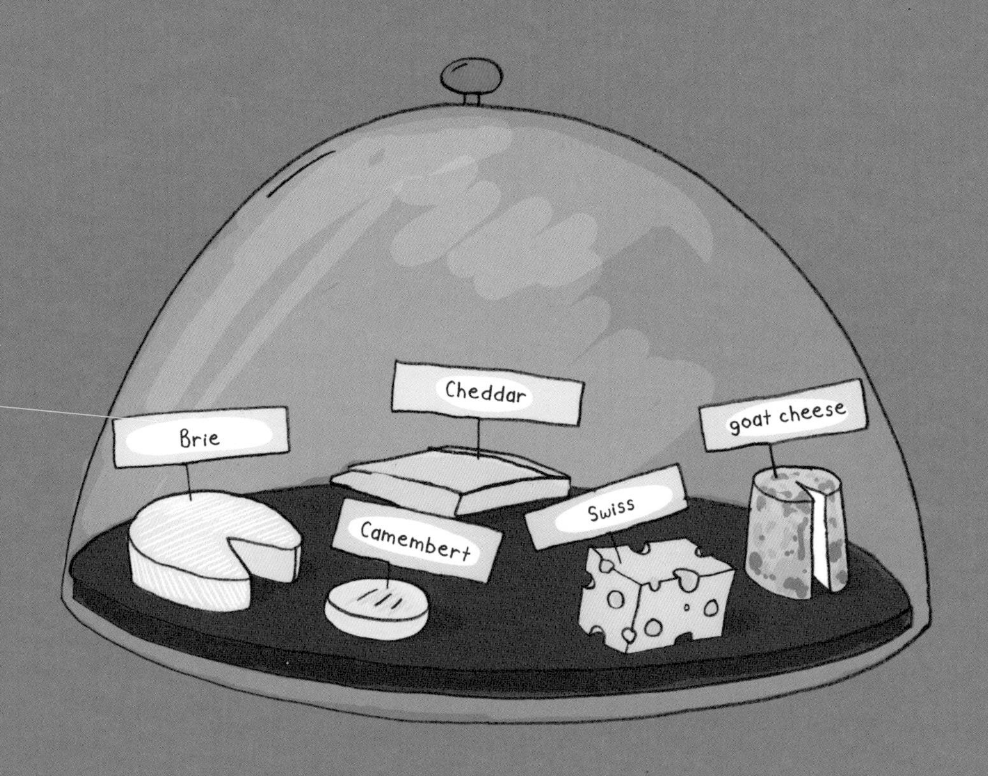

cheese

pudding

fruit yogurt

plain yogurt

chocolate mousse

dessert

banana

tangerine

apple

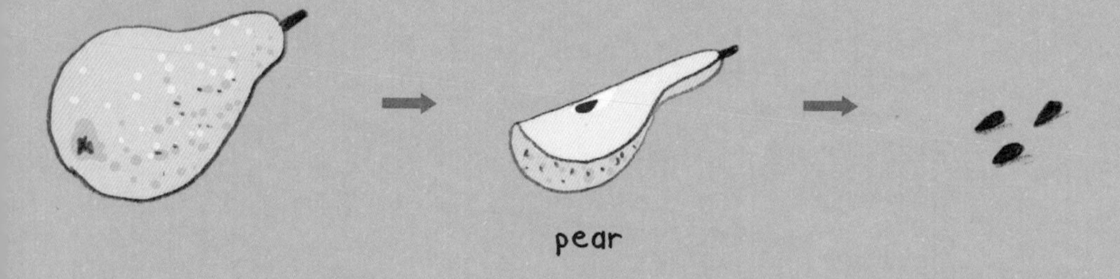
pear

peach

grapes

cherry

apricot

helping Daddy

Let's go outside...

caterpillar

butterfly

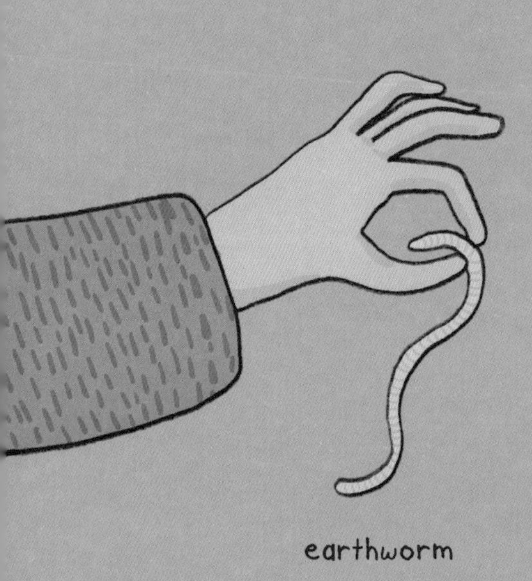

earthworm

spider

ladybug

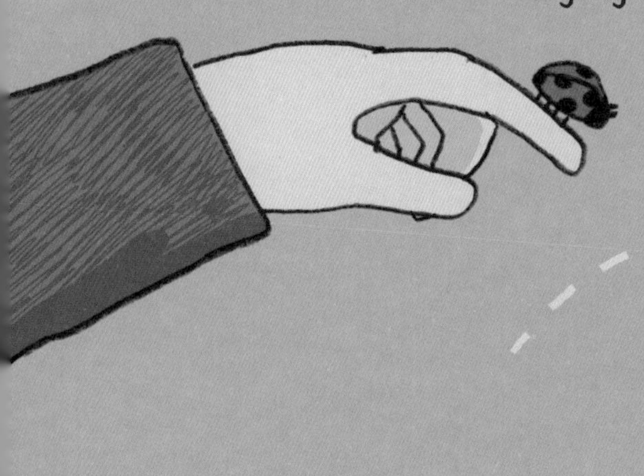

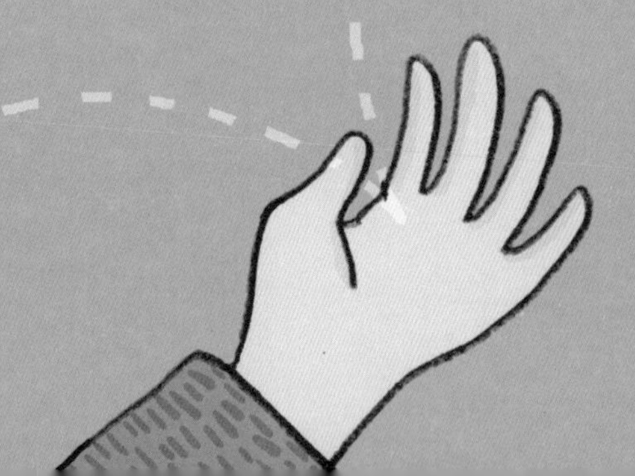

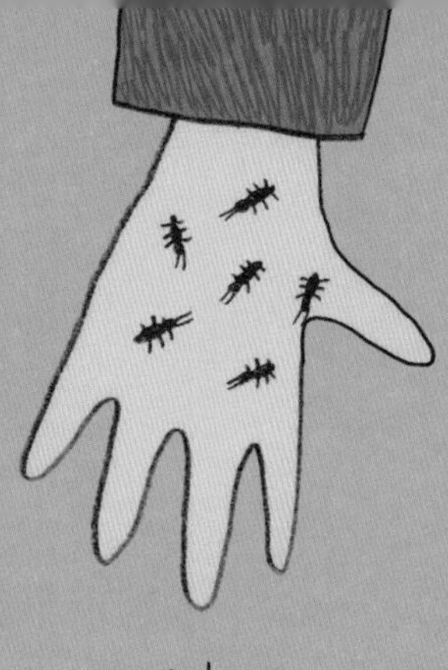
ants

grasshopper

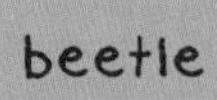
beetle

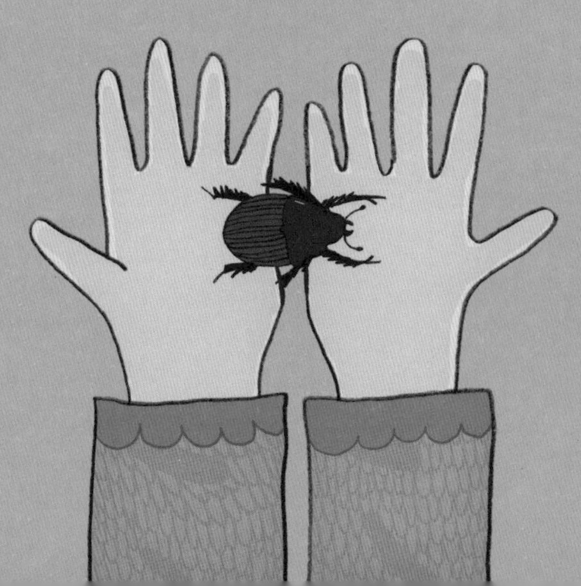

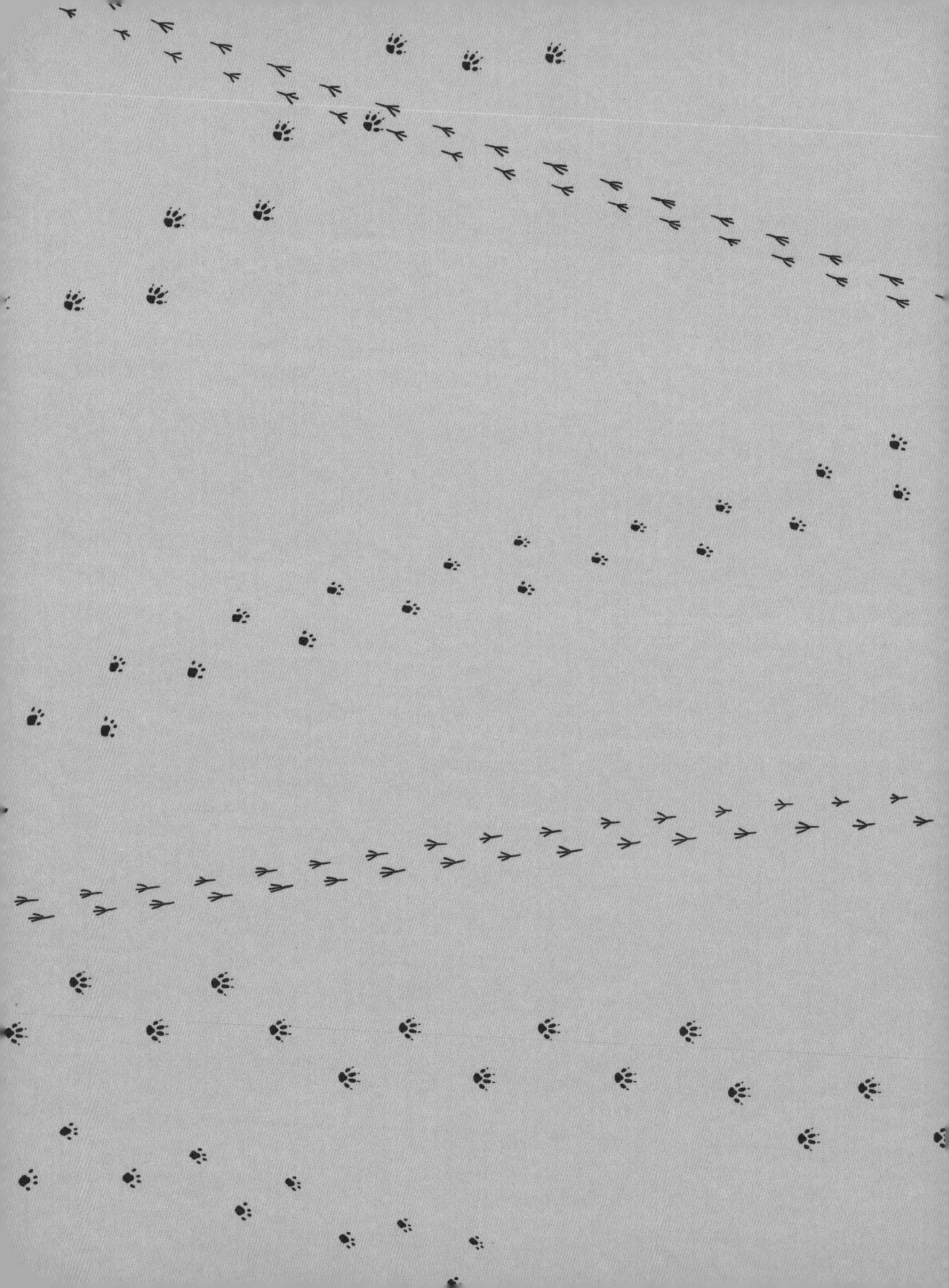

bird

cat
dog

playing in the stream

duck
picnic basket

poppy
bluebell
pansy
daisy
flowers

smelling the roses

sun hat

baseball hat

straw hat

sunglasses

tank top

shorts

sandals

summer clothes

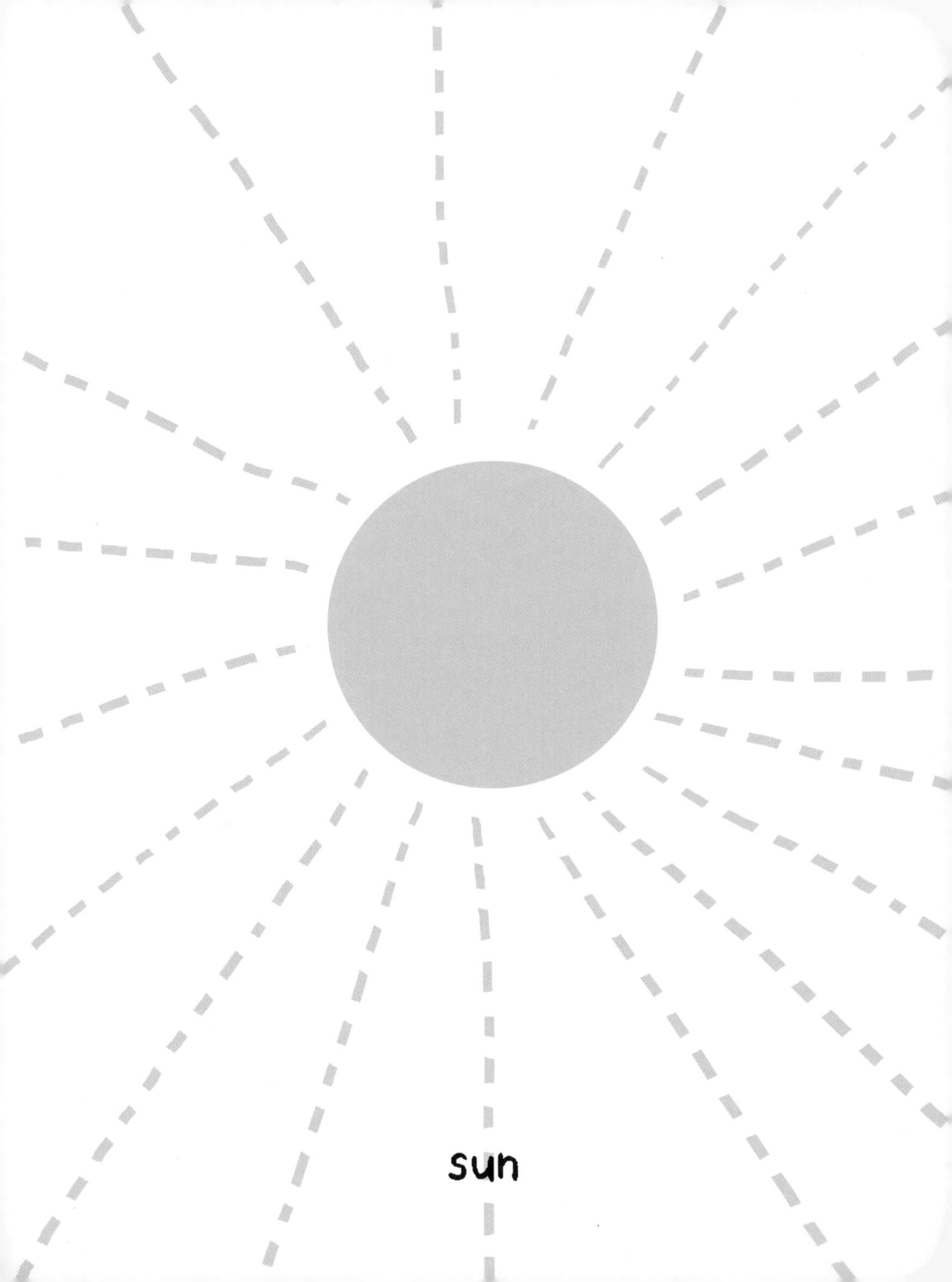
sun

at the beach

sailboat

ocean
beach umbrella
beach towel
net
rake
shovel
crab

rain

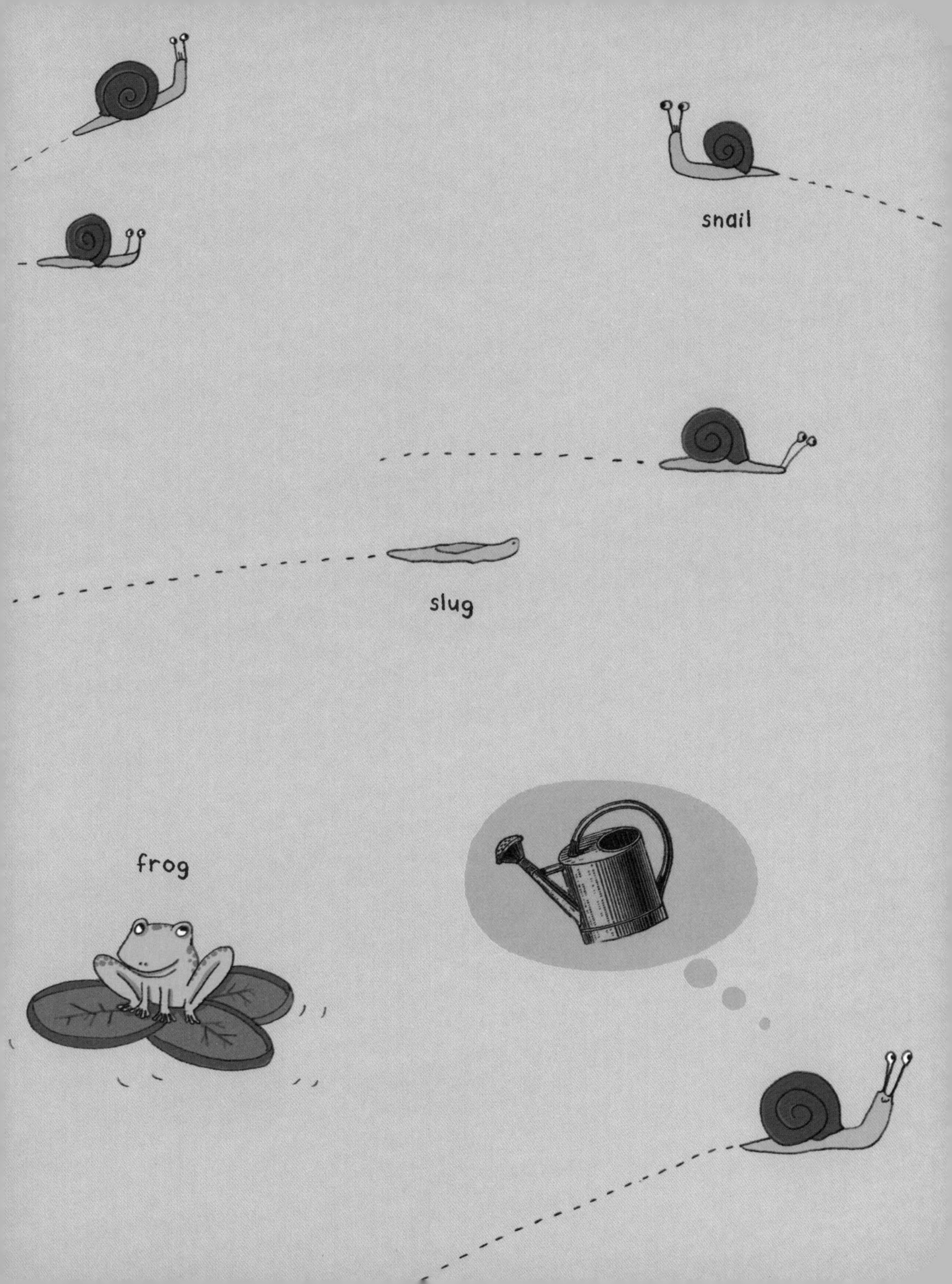
snail
slug
frog

umbrella

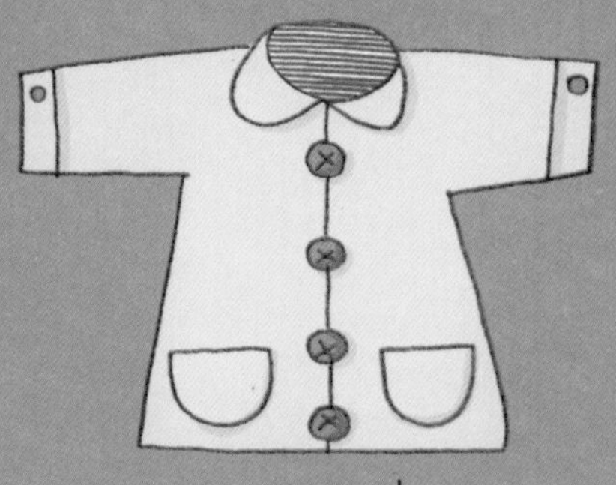

raincoat

rubber boots

rain clothes

listening to the wind

tree

scrapbook

basket of mushrooms

snowflakes

snowman

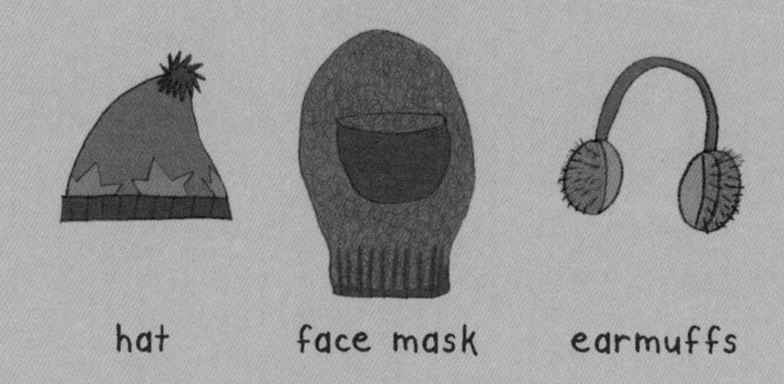

winter clothes

sled

evergreen trees

We have an idea!

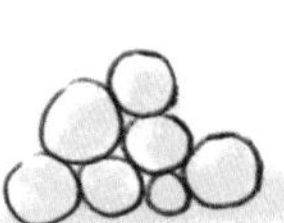

Look out!

in the cold

nice and warm

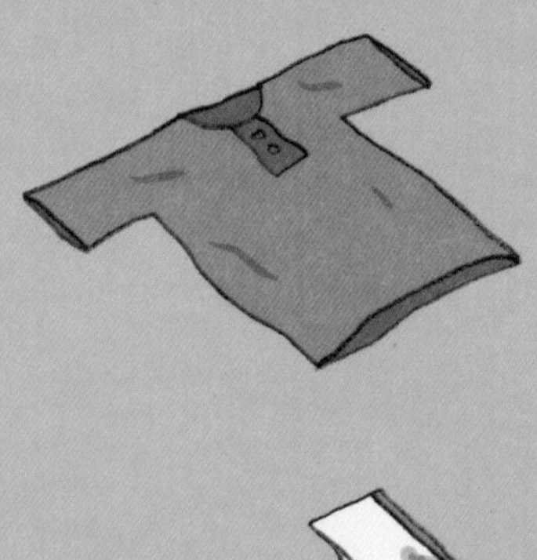

Bath time...

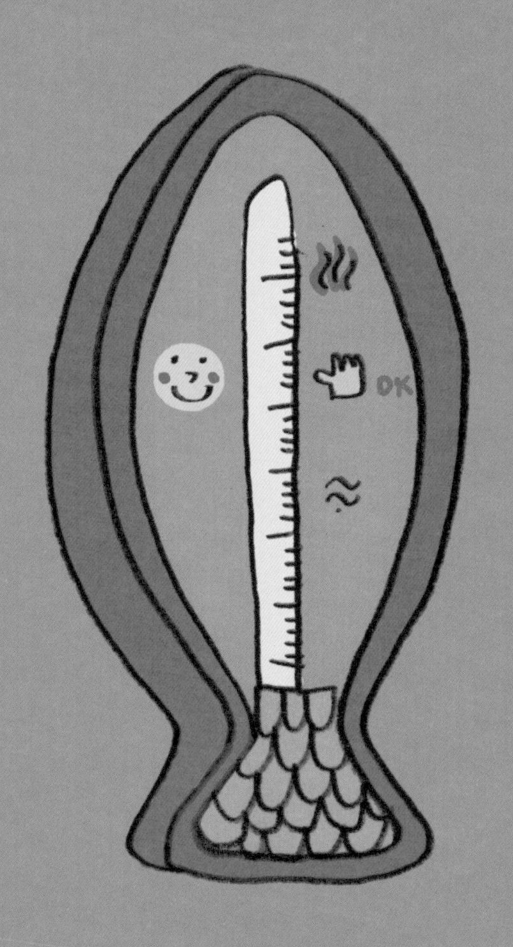

thermometer

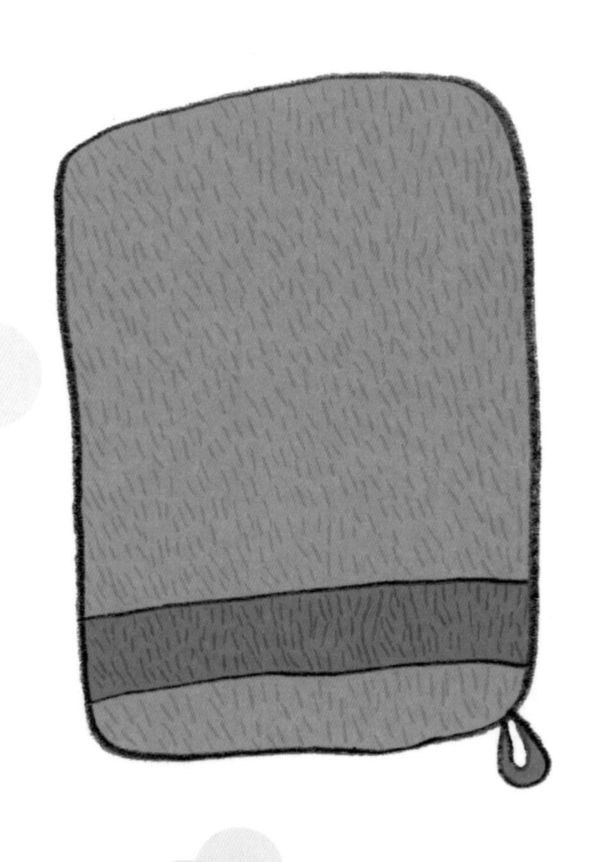

washcloth

soap

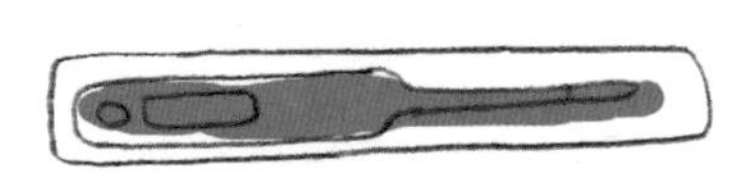

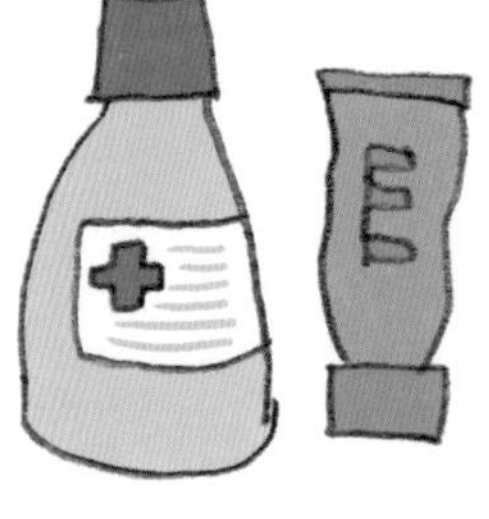

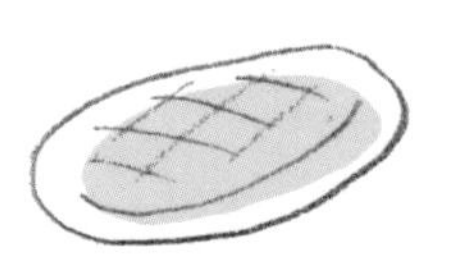

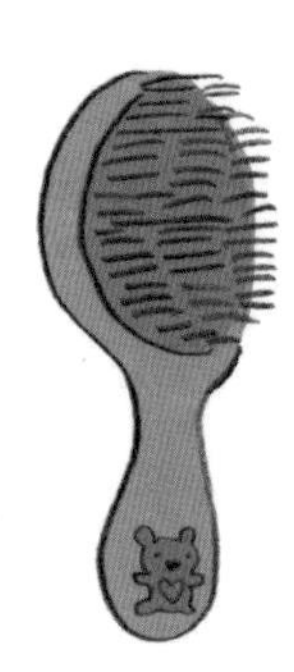

toothbrush

SPRAY

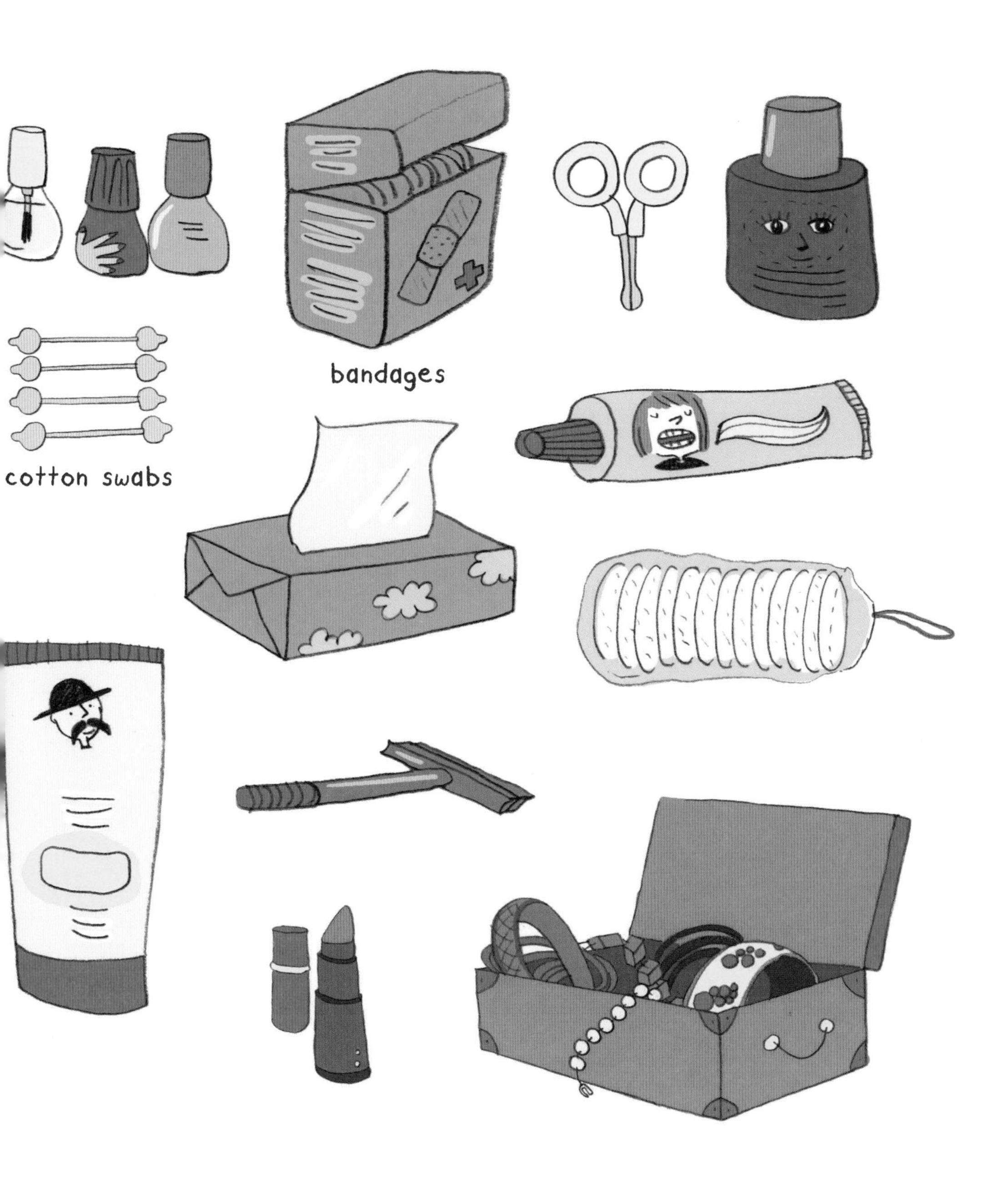

in the bathroom

bath towel

bath cape
bathrobe

hair dryer

moon

shooting star

In the moonlight...

family
dinner

acting silly

watching television

bedtime story

snuggle time

Good night!

Good night!